BOOK CLUB EDITION

WALT DISNEY'S

THE
Sorcerer's
Apprentice

Random House 🏠 New York

Copyright © 1 9 7 3 by The Walt Disney Company. All rights reserved under Inter-
national and Pan-American Copyright Conventions. Published in the United States
by Random House, Inc., New York, and simultaneously in Canada by Random House
of Canada Limited, Toronto.
Library of Congress Cataloging in Publication Data
Disney (Walt) Productions.
Walt Disney's The sorcerer's apprentice.
(Disney's wonderful world of reading, #12)
Apprenticed to a sorcerer, Mickey Mouse tries to save himself work by making some
magic.
[1. Magic—Fiction] I. Title: The sorcerer's apprentice. PZ8.W192 [E] 73-9891
ISBN 0-394-82551-9   ISBN 0-394-92551-3 (lib. bdg.)
Manufactured in the United States of America

Once there was a man who knew
everything there was to know
about magic.

He was a great sorcerer.

The sorcerer had a wonderful hat.
When he wore his hat,
he could just think magic
and it would happen.

He could think about a butterfly
and it would appear.

But only the sorcerer
knew the magic words
to make it disappear.

The sorcerer did not live alone.
He had a helper named Mickey.
Mickey did all the work.

He swept the floor.

He chopped the wood.

He carried the water
from the well.

Mickey knew about the magic of the hat.
"If I had that hat," said Mickey,
"I would never have to
work again."

One day the sorcerer had to go out.
Mickey was alone at last.
And there on the table
was the sorcerer's magic hat.

"Now I can be a sorcerer,"
said Mickey.

He reached for
the magic hat.

He put the hat on his head.

An old broom was standing by the wall.
"I will put a spell on that broom,"
said Mickey.

He did what the sorcerer always did.
He pointed his fingers at the broom.
The broom began to move.

The broom grew two feet.

It grew a right arm

and then a left arm.

"Broom!" commanded Mickey.
"Pick up the buckets."
The broom did just what Mickey said.

"Go up the steps," said Mickey.
The broom went up the steps.

"Fill the buckets," said Mickey.
The broom filled the buckets.

"Bring them back," said Mickey.
The broom brought them back.

"Pour the water," said Mickey.
The broom poured the water.

Mickey danced around the room.

"Magic is easy," he cried.

"I will never work again."

Then Mickey sat down in the sorcerer's chair.
"Work, broom, work!" he said.

While the broom went on filling buckets
and pouring water, Mickey fell asleep.

He dreamed he was the greatest
sorcerer in the world.

Suddenly something cold and wet woke him up.
It was a splash of water.

Another splash knocked Mickey
out of the chair.

Water was everywhere!
The broom was flooding the room.

"Stop!" cried Mickey.
"Stop, broom! Stop, I say!"

But the broom did not stop.

Mickey pointed his finger at the broom.
But the broom kept going.

He held out his arms.
But the broom pushed him down.

He grabbed the bucket.
But the broom held on tight.

Wasn't there any way to stop the broom?

The ax! Mickey grabbed it.

He chopped the broom into bits.
"Well, that's over!" said Mickey.

But it wasn't over.
Something strange was going on.

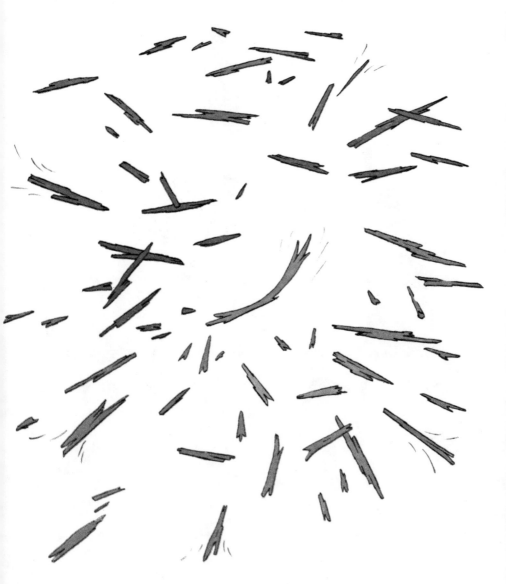

The bits of wood began to move.

The bits of wood turned into brooms.
All the new brooms had feet and arms and buckets.

They marched up the steps, never stopping.

The brooms
came back
with more water.

Mickey leaned against the door
to keep them out.

But the brooms pushed it open.

Mickey held out his arms
to hold them back.

But the brooms walked right over him.
"I am a sorcerer!" cried Mickey.
"You must do as I say."
But the brooms marched on and on.

Brooms and more brooms!
Buckets and more buckets!
In a great line,
they poured
and poured.

The water got deeper and deeper.
Poor Mickey!
It was all he could do
to keep his head above the water.

Then the sorcerer's Book of Magic
floated by.

Mickey grabbed it.

Page after page after page...
Mickey looked for the magic words
that would stop the brooms.

But the water began to whirl.
Mickey couldn't read the words.

Mickey hung onto the book
as he went around and around
in the water.

Spinning faster and faster,
Mickey was caught
in a great whirlpool.
Now there was nothing
he could do.

But what was this?
A great dark shadow on the wall!
The sorcerer had come back.

He knew at once what Mickey had done.

He raised his arms
and roared a great command.

The brooms and the water
disappeared.
Just one broom was left.
It was the old broom
standing by the wall.

The sorcerer was frowning.
He looked down at Mickey.

Mickey took off the sorcerer's hat.

Very carefully,
ever so neatly,
he made it look
nice again.

Then he gave the hat back to the sorcerer.
"Just a little magic trick, ha, ha!"
said Mickey.
But the sorcerer did not laugh.

The sorcerer looked down
at his little helper.

"Don't start what you can't finish,"
he said.

So Mickey went up the steps
and back to work.